The Fox

A PLAY

by **Allan Miller**

Based on the short novel
The Fox

by **D. H. Lawrence**

A SAMUEL FRENCH ACTING EDITION

SAMUEL FRENCH

FOUNDED 1830

New York Hollywood London Toronto

SAMUELFRENCH.COM

THE FOX was first presented by the Back Alley Theatre in Los Angeles, April 4, 1981. It was produced by Laura Zucker and directed by Allan Miller. Lighting was by Christopher Milliken, costumes by Hilary Sloane. Production Stage Manager was Michael Wymore.

CAST

(In Order of Appearance)

NELLIE MARCH . . . . *Jenny O'Hara*

JILL BANFORD . . . . *Margaret Ladd*

HENRY GRENFEL. . . . . *Michael Horton*

The first New York production of THE FOX was at the Roundabout Theatre Company, Gene Feist and Michael Fried, Producing Directors, on July 7, 1982. Allan Miller directed. Scene Design was by Roger Mooney, Costume Design by A. Christina Giannini, Lighting Design by Ronald Wallace, and Sound Design by Philip Campanella.

THE CAST

(In Order of Appearance)

NELLIE MARCH . . . . *Jenny O'Hara*

JILL BANFORD . . . . *Mary Layne*

HENRY GRENFEL . . . . *Anthony Heald*

CHARACTERS

JILL BANFORD---nearly thirty. A small achey creature.

NELLIE MARCH---nearly thirty. Tall and strong-looking.

HENRY GRENFEL---twenty. A soldier. Fair and lean.

The time of the play is November, 1918. The scene is the old Bailey Farm, England. The farm is a modest affair, and so is the house in which the girls live. Nothing is ramshackle, but neither is there any sign of prosperity. The colors inside the house are warm, but with only the fire and one or two lamps to light the place the rooms crawl with dark spots and shadows.

PRODUCTION NOTE

The symbolism of Henry as The Fox, so wonderfully wrought, so early on, in the D.H. Lawrence novella, must be allowed to develop ever so subtly and gradually in this dramatization.

I have written Henry here as a truly innocent woods spirit whose predatory instincts come into play well before his consciousness can define them. He is finely curious of these two women on the farm. He's never met creatures like them. He admires their boldness in trying to live their lives separate from the demands of the town cultures they've moved away from, but he also recognizes their lack of knowledge and the quick-wittedness necessary to survival on their terms.

So his first actions toward them are generous, engaging, even mischievous, but not in any way possessive. Only as he begins to draw out Nellie's inner needs and desires, and fancies, does his predatory nature assert itself. Even so, till almost the very end, he is still willing to sacrifice some of his own aspirations to achieve his soul-mating with Nellie. His offer to get a job, and his offer to stay on with Nellie and Jill after he and Nellie are married, are meant as testimony to his need for her. It is Jill's instincts that lead her to perceive what Henry is really up to and capable of.

ALSO

I've written in an auto-harp for Jill to play. Any similar instrument will do. Even a piano.

THE FOX may be performed with one intermission by playing Act II & III without a break.

5

The Fox

ACT ONE

SCENE One

*The stage has two playing areas, the parlor, and
Stage Left of it, a raised area that is the woodshed.
The parlor contains a fireplace far Stage Right, with
two rough but comfortable armchairs in front of it.
Upstage Right is a doorway leading to the kitchen.
Stage Left—Upstage of the back wall of the
woodshed—is the front door of the house. Just
Upstage of the front door and Stage Right of it are
the stairs leading to the second floor. Immediately
Downstage of the front door is a blanket chest.
Upstage Center is a marble topped sideboard with
bottom cabinets tucked in under the stairwell. To
the Right of the sideboard are several bookshelves,
obviously handmade. In the woodshed, in the
Center of the space, is a tree stump that is used for
sawing logs.*

*It is a brisk November evening, dark, and the wind
very much alive.* JILL *is in a chair by the fire, a
shawl wrapped around her shoulders, playing her
auto-harp.* NELLIE *is at a small work table with the
kerosene lamp for light, working out a design on a
porcelain vase, wearing her breeches and boots, and
a sweater.*

NELLIE *smiles at* JILL. JILL *crosses to her.*

NELLIE. What is it?

JILL. I miss you. (*They laugh.* NELLIE *turns back to her painting. A single dog barks off in the distance.* NELLIE *reacts sharply.* JILL *puts her hand steadyingly on* NELLIE's *shoulder.* NELLIE *reaches up to touch her hand.*)

NELLIE. You get back to the fire. You'll catch a chill. (JILL *moves back to her chair. The single dog is now joined by a group of others, all excited.*)

JILL. They sound as though they've found something.

NELLIE. Sshh.

JILL. What do you think it is?

NELLIE. Sshh! (*The dog sounds become louder, seeming very close.* NELLIE *hurries to the door and flings it open.*)

JILL. Nellie! (NELLIE *swings around to face* JILL. *The dogs suddenly move further away.*) It's cold. Close the door . . . ! (NELLIE *closes the door. The dog sounds gradually disappear.*) What do you think it was? Hm . . . ? Nellie!

NELLIE. What?

JILL. What did you think that was?

NELLIE. I don't know.

JILL. Then why did you jump so?

NELLIE. I didn't jump.

JILL. You flew! What were you afraid of?

NELLIE. Don't be silly.

JILL. I know when you're frightened and when you're not.

NELLIE. I wasn't frightened . . . ! Do you want the lamp now, I'm not going to paint anymore.

JILL. Nellie!

NELLIE. What?

JILL. What did you think that was?

NELLIE. Nothing!

JILL. What did you think that was? What have you been thinking about . . . ! Do you know you've been moaning in your sleep?

NELLIE. I have?

JILL. And you've cried out twice?

NELLIE. When was that?

JILL. Last was Saturday night.

NELLIE. What did I say?

JILL. Nothing. But your face was wet and your hands were cold. You sat up when you called out but I talked to you and you lay back down again. What were you dreaming about, Nellie? Tell me.

NELLIE. I was dreaming the water turned cold in the middle of a bath, you cuckoo. Is that what you're so bothered about?

JILL. Nellie—

NELLIE. What?

JILL. Winter is coming—

NELLIE. It always does.

JILL. The chickens won't lay, the barn's falling down . . .

NELLIE. The barn'll be mended.

JILL. The house is getting cold again, and my shoulder's always hurting . . .

NELLIE. Ohh—

JILL. The fox is stealing all our hens, and we never have enough money! How are we going to feed ourselves when the ground's dried up and we can't even draw out a vegetable? My mum was right, we'll never last another winter!

NELLIE. Yes we will.

JILL. How can we? How can we? We've got to face up to it, we're losing here, Nellie. We're not living the life we hoped for in this empty house, with not enough food

and never enough time for all the things that have got to
be done. Why can't we visit somewhere 'till we're settled
and calm again?

NELLIE. Where?

JILL. We could go to my place.

NELLIE. And do what?

JILL. Anything we like. We wouldn't be tied to the
house. And my brother Jack's coming home soon. We
could do so many things with him. And we could always
come out here again next summer!

NELLIE. If we leave now you know we'll never come
back.

JILL. Yes we will.

NELLIE. This is what we planned for. This is what we
chose.

JILL. But nothing's working out properly.

NELLIE. We came here to live our own lives, didn't
we? Without having to strut about to other people's
ideas, and other people's demands —

JILL. But look what's happening to us now . . . ! (*She
accidentally knocks the porcelain vase that* NELLIE *was
painting to the floor.*)

NELLIE. It's only a piece of porcelain . . . We haven't
had any flowers to put in it since September . . . ! (JILL
*bends to the floor to help pick up the pieces. Suddenly
there is a sharp crack of a twig in the yard.*)

JILL. Nellie, someone's out there. It may be a tramp!

NELLIE. Turn down the light.

JILL. Get the gun.

NELLIE. Turn down the light!

JILL. Get the gun! (*As* NELLIE *rushes into the kitchen
for the shotgun there is a knock at the door.*)

NELLIE. Who is it? (*Instead of a reply the door opens*

and HENRY *appears, in uniform, with a pack on his back. He smiles as* NELLIE *levels the gun at him.*)

HENRY. Hello!

NELLIE. What do you want here?

HENRY. Why, what's wrong?

NELLIE. What do you want here? Speak up or I shall shoot!

HENRY. Why I've come to see my grand-dad.

NELLIE. Who is your grand-dad? Who is he?

HENRY. William Grenfel.

NELLIE. There's no William Grenfel lives here.

HENRY. There isn't?

NELLIE. You know there isn't. Now move away or I shall shoot!

HENRY. I lived here with my grand-dad five years ago. What's become of him then?

JILL. There was an old man lived here before us, Nellie. He lived all alone.

HENRY. Ay, that's him. What's become of him then?

JILL. We were told he died.

HENRY. Ayy, that's where he is.

NELLIE. How is it you didn't know if your grand-dad was alive or dead?

HENRY. I joined up in Canada, you see. That's where I ran away to. I hadn't heard from him in three or four years.

JILL. We've been here almost three years.

HENRY. Have you?

JILL. Nellie, put up the gun. Mr Grenfel's a visitor.

HENRY. Ay, we've seen enough of guns.

JILL. Nellie . . . ! (*She gestures for* NELLIE *to lower the gun.*) Would you like to sit down a bit, Mr. Grenfel? Have you come from very far?

HENRY. Salonika.

JILL. Salonika? I have a brother coming home from France.

HENRY. Coming here?

JILL. No, going to his house, in Islington, where my family lives.

HENRY. I know the town.

JILL. Do you? My dad owns a clothing shop there.

HENRY. Does he? What's his name?

HENRY. Banford. Brawleigh Banford.

HENRY. Is that the name of the shop?

JILL. No. "Woolens" . . . ! Would you like a cup of tea, Mr. Grenfel? To take the chill off?

HENRY. Thank you I would, Miss Banford.

NELLIE. I'll get it.

JILL. No, no, I will, Nellie — (*But* NELLIE *has crossed into the kitchen before her, with the gun.*) Well there's no need of the two of us for a pot of water. Did you come in on the train, Mr. Grenfel? (*She gestures* HENRY *to the chair she occupied at the fire.*)

HENRY. Yes I did. (JILL *hurries to the chair to remove the harp before* HENRY *sits, and leaves the kerosene lamp on the fireplace mantel.*)

JILL. And then you walked the whole way out here?

HENRY. Ay.

JILL. You must be tired then.

HENRY. A little.

JILL. Were you planning to live here with your grand dad again?

HENRY. Until I'm sent to Canada. I'm on leave now.

JILL. Where will you stay then? How long have you got? (*She places her harp in the cabinet part of the sideboard.*)

HENRY. Oh I know some people in the village. I can always stay at the Swan.

JILL. The Swan's quarantined with the influenza. It's brought down half the town by now.

HENRY. Has it?

JILL. I'm sure it has.

HENRY. Is that why you stay out here? Afraid of catching the flu?

JILL. We've had lots worse than that, Mr. Grenfel.

HENRY. Have you?

JILL. Our first year here I caught pneumonia.

HENRY. Did you?

JILL. I was bedded down for a fortnight. I came to this place for my health, but it hasn't improved any yet, believe me.

HENRY. And what has Nellie caught since she's been here?

JILL. Nothing. She's never sick. That's why I've got to make it up for the two of us. (*She sits in the downstage chair by the fire.*)

HENRY. But you said you've both had worse than the flu.

JILL. Well wouldn't you call mending coops and chasing chicks and chopping wood and draining ditches from twelve to fourteen hours a day at least as much as catching the flu?

HENRY. Yes I would.

JILL. Well Nellie does more.

HENRY. Does she? (NELLIE *comes in, carrying a tray of food.*)

JILL. Don't you Nellie?

NELLIE. Are you chattering about me?

JILL. I was just telling Mr. Grenfel that . . .

HENRY. Henry—

JILL. Henry. How you do all the heavy work, and I do all the bed watching.

NELLIE. Tea'll be a minute. There's nothing but bread and margerine and jam to chew, I'm afraid.

HENRY. A bit of bread'll taste quite a lot just now, Miss Nellie. Thank you. (NELLIE *crosses into the kitchen again.*)

JILL. How long since you've eaten, Henry?

HENRY. Since noon today.

JILL. Since noon? That's a terrible stretch for a growing boy. You gobble this then and I'll slice you another.

HENRY. Thank you.

JILL. I'm just so sorry we haven't got a chunk of meat to go with it. Food's been awful scarce in the village with the rationing, and we've had little luck in the woods on our own.

HENRY. Hunting used to be good out there.

JILL. It still is, but we haven't got the time and we haven't got the patience. There's all the feeding and weeding, and mending and cleaning, and oh, there's never an end to what has to be done out here. Well you know about that.

HENRY. What kind of stock do you have beside the chickens?

JILL. We've got ducks, and a horse, and a heifer — No, we had a heifer. We had to sell her.

HENRY. Why?

JILL. She was always crashing fences, and then she got herself pregnant . . . Well, we're not out here to slave our lives away. Heifers are always trouble, so we had to sell her . . . ! Nellie, what are you up to out there?

NELLIE. (*OFF.*) I had to build the fire from scratch.

JILL. Well why didn't you set it on in here . . . ? Nellie makes a fine pot of tea, Henry, you'll enjoy it.

HENRY. You make a fine slice of bread.

JILL. Does it feel good?

HENRY. It's like a heaven sent gift to my poor aching body. My grand-dad would have had me out dragging in wood for the week by now.

JILL. On your first night back?

HENRY. Ay.

JILL. Is that why you left him?

HENRY. That, and the cut of his tongue. He had a way of making the sun seem cold.

JILL. He sounds terrible.

HENRY. Terrible he was. He brought me here when I was twelve years old, and . . .

JILL. How long did you stay?

HENRY. Till I was fifteen.

JILL. And you left five years ago. That makes you twenty in all. My brother's twenty-one!

HENRY. He'll come home an old man then, won't he . . . ? You've done a wondrous thing in here, Jill. My grand dad kept this room a cellar bin. The walls were always bare, the floor was always black . . . (NELLIE *comes in with the tea.*)

JILL. Here we are.

NELLIE. You pour out, Jill.

JILL. Of course, don't I always . . . ? You see a difference in the room, do you Henry? (NELLIE *crosses to the blanket chest near the door, and sits on it.*)

HENRY. Don't I though?

JILL. I put up the curtains and I found the furniture. Nellie put up the shelves, but I brought in most of the books.

HENRY. I like to read.

JILL. I love it, but my eyes can't always take the strain. Nellie's a great reader too, but lately she's become most fond of filigree work on porcelain, these cups are hers . . . (JILL *crosses to* NELLIE *with her tea.*)

JILL. She's done pitchers and vases, and lots of others.

HENRY. Your handiwork is lovely, Nellie. Very.

JILL. Say thank you, Nellie.

NELLIE. Thank you.

JILL. Come sit by the fire, Nellie, where it's warm.

NELLIE. I'm all right.

HENRY. But we can't see you.

NELLIE. I can see you . . . ! (JILL *crosses back to pour her own tea.*)

HENRY. Well you've both made a little dream world out here in the forest, ladies, take my word.

NELLIE. You haven't seen the outside.

HENRY. What?

NELLIE. You haven't seen the outside.

HENRY. The outside needs sturdying up, and so does the barn, but a good hand could clear that up in a wink.

JILL. Nellie is a good hand, but this place takes more clearing than she can do.

HENRY. Why have you never taken anybody on then?

JILL. We did once, but he turned out to be more worthless than the hens.

HENRY. What's wrong with your hens?

JILL. Tell him, Nellie. (*She and* NELLIE *laugh.*)

HENRY. What?

NELLIE. Go on.

JILL. (*Still laughing.*) They won't lay! When we give them hot food in the morning they flop out for hours in a trance, and when we give them their hot food at night they peck about like a pack of sleepwalkers in all the early hours of the day! And then when the government passed the Daylight Savings Bill the stupid birds refused to go to sleep until nine o'clock or later, and that spoiled them. Now they click and clack about all day and all night like a bunch of wacky clocks . . . It's no laughing matter!

HENRY. (*Laughing, too.*) I could get your hens to sleep. And I could get your hens to lay.

JILL. How?

HENRY. Hot food's for Wyandots. You've only got Leghorns, haven't you?

JILL. How do you know that?

HENRY. I looked . . . ! I could get your hens to lay all right. And I could sturdy your barn, and bring you in food for your kitchen.

JILL. Could you?

HENRY. Take my word.

JILL. Could you also shoot us a fox?

HENRY. I've shot more than my share before.

JILL. This one's clever. He makes us stand guard when we're too tired or too blind to catch him. Nellie saw him once, but she couldn't get a shot at him.

HENRY. What did he look like?

JILL. Nellie?

NELLIE. What?

JILL. What did the fox look like, Henry wants to know?

NELLIE. Why?

HENRY. I might know something about his habits if I knew his colors.

JILL. Tell him.

NELLIE. He has a golden brown and grayish white muzzle, with a thick white tipped tail, and with white . . . under the tail. And a thick, fiery brush all over his body.

HENRY. A "fiery" brush?

JILL. She's been dreaming about him.

HENRY. Has she?

NELLIE. Jill!

JILL. Well you have, haven't you?

HENRY. And how long has he been about?

JILL. Almost a year.

NELLIE. He came last winter.

HENRY. Always the same one?

NELLIE. Always.

HENRY. How do you know that if you've only seem him once?

NELLIE. I know.

JILL. Nellie knows, Henry. It's always the same one.

HENRY. And has he bothered any of the other farms?

JILL. Oh yes.

NELLIE. But he always come back here.

HENRY. That's because he knows you don't have a man about the place . . . ! Well farming is an all day chore. My grand dad and I never had time for curtains or filigree work.

JILL. We don't believe in living for nothing but work, Henry.

HENRY. Ay, that's it. To work a farm you might as well be a beast yourself. But if your hens won't lay, and your larder's bare, how much longer do you think you can last?

NELLIE. We shall hold on a time.

HENRY. What will you do when you've used up all your capital?

NELLIE. Hire ourselves out for landworkers, I suppose.

JILL. Or borrow another bit from my dad.

HENRY. There won't be any demand for women landworkers now the war's over. And suppose your dad was to decide to have you home again? A farm needs a man about the place, take my word . . . ! Well I better be going now or I'll find the other half of town in bed, asleep.

JILL. How long is it till your leave is up, Henry?

HENRY. A week.

JILL. And then they're shipping you back to Canada?

HENRY. That's where I want to be. First they're sending me back to camp though.

JILL. Where is that?

HENRY. Near Salisbury Plain. About sixty miles.

JILL. Do you have a home in Canada, with relations?

HENRY. I have a home with no one. I have no home, but I have the country. It's a wild place, but you've seen no more beautiful sights in this world. I've lived snowy nights and soggy days in cabins and lean-tos, and I've slept on the side of a mountain to watch the clouds rise like balloons below me. England is my birth, but Canada is my life . . . ! I thank you for your kind good thoughts, ladies, I'll be on my way now.

JILL. Henry . . . ? Suppose you find no one with a bed to spare?

HENRY. I'll trade with a horse. Goodnight.

JILL. Nellie . . . ? I'd say you could spend the night here, Henry, only . . .

HENRY. What?

JILL. Well, propriety, I suppose.

HENRY. It wouldn't be improper, would it? How could it be?

JILL. Not as far as we're concerned.

HENRY. Not as far as I'm concerned. After all, it is my own house, in a way.

JILL. It's what the village will have to say. They don't take kindly to our being out here as it is.

HENRY. They're all half sick with the flu, that's what they get from minding how you live.

JILL. Well what do you say, Nellie? Hm?

NELLIE. It's all the same to me. We can look after ourselves. (*She crosses into the kitchen with her cup.*)

HENRY. Of course you can, I've seen that.

JILL. Well then stop if you like, Henry. We have a bed for you.

HENRY. If you're sure it isn't troubling you too much.

JILL. Oh it's no trouble. It's good to have company again.

HENRY. It's awfully good not having to turn out again, take my word.

JILL. Sit yourself down then and rest, while I ready your room.

NELLIE. (*Coming back in.*) I'll tidy the room.

JILL. I'll do it, Nellie. You stay and build the fire up . . . ! We have two rooms, Henry. Would you rather face the sun or the shade? (*She takes the lamp from the mantel and moves to the stairs.*)

HENRY. Either.

JILL. Not that there'll be much sun for you to see this time of the year.

HENRY. I'll take the shady one then.

JILL. I'll give you the sunny one, it's brighter . . . ! Oh, and would you like to scrub up tonight before turning in? I can run a tub for you if you want?

HENRY. Ay, I'd like that.

JILL. I'll heat the water for you soon as I've done upstairs.

NELLIE. I'll get the water.

JILL. You sit, Nellie, you've done enough today. I'll be down in a jiff . . . ! (*She hurries up the stairs with the lamp.* NELLIE *crosses out the door and returns in a moment with some logs. As she moves to the fire* HENRY *gets up behind her, and touches her on the shoulder.*)

HENRY. Can I help you with that, Nellie? (NELLIE *almost cries out.*) What is it, did I frighten you?

NELLIE. No.

HENRY. I'm sorry if I did.

NELLIE. You didn't . . . ! (*She stoops to the fire again.* JILL *appears again.*)

JILL. Henry, I forgot to ask, do you use a pillow? We have two extra.

HENRY. One will be fine, Jill. Thank you.

JILL. I'll give you the fluffy one then . . . ! Henry, why don't you come and unpack now, then you'll be all settled for the night after your tub. Do you want to do that? Hm?

HENRY. Ay.

JILL. You come along too, Nellie. We can talk up here . . . ! (*She disappears again.*)

HENRY. Are you coming, Nellie?

NELLIE. In a minute.

HENRY. Hurry . . . ! (*He smiles at her, and then climbs the stairs.* NELLIE *stares after him, and . . .*)

THE LIGHTS FADE

SCENE TWO

Early morning. The parlor is still dark. A light can be seen at the head of the stairs.

JILL. (*OFF.*) Henry? Henry . . . ?

NELLIE. (*OFF.*) Go on down. (JILL *comes down the stairs and* NELLIE *follows.*)

JILL. Henry . . . ? He isn't here. (NELLIE *opens the door.*) Do you see anything?

NELLIE. Dark woods and a tipsy barn. The logs need piling. (*She closes the door and crosses to the fire.*)

JILL. Nellie, aren't you concerned about him?

NELLIE. What shall I do?

JILL. Call him.

NELLIE. Why?

JILL. I want to know if he's left us or he hasn't.

NELLIE. Then you call him . . . !

JILL. Well you're in a nice state this morning.

NELLIE. You'd like a fire, wouldn't you?

JILL. Yes.

NELLIE. Then I've got to clear away the ashes, haven't I?

JILL. Suppose something's happened to him?

NELLIE. He looks as if he could manage.

JILL. Nellie!

NELLIE. What?

JILL. What's happened to you? Don't his whereabouts concern you at all? This is his first day here. Where could he be? What could he be doing?

NELLIE. Perhaps he took a walk.

JILL. Why?

NELLIE. Why not?

JILL. I don't know. But why wouldn't you call out for him then? What happened to you last night, did you dream again?

NELLIE. Did you hear me get out of bed?

JILL. No! Why? Did you . . . ? Hm?

NELLIE. I thought I heard someone singing outside the window.

JILL. Singing? Who?

NELLIE. The fox!

JILL. The fox?

NELLIE. The singing went all round the house and out into the fields. I had to get up to make sure. He was out there, in the yard, right at my feet, looking up at me. And I wanted to touch him but when I stretched out my hand, he bit me. Right through the wrist. And then he whisked his brush against my mouth. And it burned . . . ! Then he made off, laughing . . . I'm not a staring post, Jill. You've dreamt queer things haven't you?

JILL. Nothing as queer as that.

NELLIE. I've felt you snuggle round me in the middle of a night.

JILL. Because I was cold.

NELLIE. You've got your water bottle to keep you warm.

JILL. You know it doesn't last but a little time.

NELLIE. Listen now! I'm telling you what I saw and heard in my sleep . . .

JILL. All right.

NELLIE. It was a trick. That's what dreaming is, isn't it? We see at night what we can never even imagine during the day . . .

JILL. All right, Nellie.

NELLIE. But if I can't even confide in you anymore what's the good of things between us?

JILL. I'm sorry, I'm sorry . . . ! (HENRY *suddenly enters carrying the gun, two pheasants on a thong, and some eggs in his pockets.*)

HENRY. Did I wake you while I was in the woods? I went out deep so . . .

NELLIE. Must you break in here like that? Without a knock, or even a cough? You're a soldier and you've traveled, but you haven't learned any manners yet, have you?

JILL. Nellie.

HENRY. I beg your pardon.

NELLIE. (*Crossing to him.*) And what are you doing with my gun.

HENRY. I thought you might like . . .

NELLIE. Put it down and leave it down! (*She takes the gun and puts it in the kitchen.*)

HENRY. I'm sorry, Nellie. I didn't think to ask.

JILL. What's that you're carrying Henry, pheasants?

HENRY. For your table. And here's what your hens have done this morning.

JILL. Ohh, Henry.

HENRY. I'll round you up a dozen more before suntime.

JILL. How in the world . . . Our hens never lay before noon.

HENRY. They do now.

JILL. That's why we've always had to put aside an egg or two for breakfast! Nellie, look what a good wind Henry's brought us. And how in the world did you ever get the pheasants? They're usually so quick Nellie can never get a sight on them!

HENRY. They were just sailing into the wood when I caught them!

JILL. They must have been sailing fast with wings like these. Nellie, come look! You must be a golden shot, Henry. Where did you pick that up, during the war?

HENRY. Before the war, when I was here with my grand dad. (NELLIE *comes from the kitchen with some small branches for the living room fireplace.*)

JILL. Well the practice was good for the pudding. You just wait and see what I'm going to make us out of all this. We have enough here to entertain Lloyd George and the palace guard now, don't we Nellie? Don't we?

NELLIE. (*At the fireplace.*) Yes, we do.

JILL. We thank you for the treat, Henry. There'll be feasting and no fasting at the Old Bailey Farm tonight!

HENRY. I'll take them out and trim them up for you.

JILL. No, no.

NELLIE. I'll do that.

JILL. Nellie'll do it, Henry.

HENRY. You must have lots else to do, don't you Nellie?

NELLIE. Not so much that I can't manage these.

HENRY. I have a way with these creatures though. So let me trim them for you, can't I?

NELLIE. I have a way with them too, Henry. I'd rather trim them myself.

HENRY. Why would you when I've offered?

NELLIE. Because it's my job. You've done the hunting.

HENRY. Is that why?

NELLIE. Yes it is. Let me have them.

HENRY. Let me, Nellie.

NELLIE. Give them to me.

HENRY. I want them, Nellie. Please?

JILL. Let him have them, Nellie. They're his to do with.

NELLIE. Have them then. Have them! There's more wood to bring in and I've no time for talking . . . ! (*She crosses out through the kitchen. We hear the door slam.*)

HENRY. Your partner's got queer streaks in her, hasn't she Jill? She likes to beat her own path, doesn't she? Like a big, dark bird.

JILL. You're not one to hedge either, Henry.

HENRY. I hope I didn't make her mad though. Do you think I did?

JILL. No, not Nellie. She never minds anything much. She'll carry around a bother about as long as I can milk a cow.

HENRY. How long is that?

JILL. From here to here . . . ! You do what you have to then, while I poach us some breakfast.

HENRY. Jill.

JILL. Yes?

HENRY. Why does she always wear men's clothing, though? Doesn't she like to think of her figure?

JILL. She's got dresses. For the summer time.

HENRY. Has she.

JILL. She only wears what she does now for all the mucky work, and the weather.

HENRY. I like women to wear dresses all year round. Ladies ought to look like ladies that's what I think. Like you do. Like a little white flower. That's the way a man wants to see you, take my word . . . ! Well I'll tend to these two and then I'll chase out your fowl. Where do you keep their feed, in the barn?

JILL. Henry no, don't you do that.

HENRY. Why not?

JILL. You're not going to spend your day handing out chicken food. It's barely six o'clock. Time you were still in bed.

HENRY. Six o'clock's an army hour too, Jill. At six in the morning I've had to be sighting on Bulgars and Huns. I'll trade your chicken feed for my rations, and killings, anytime . . . ! Now you hear me, I'm going to have those hoppers of your laying twice their load before I leave today, you see if I don't.

JILL. Henry, don't chase them out yet though. Not until we're ready to stand guard.

HENRY. Guard for what?

JILL. For the fox. We have to watch him every day or he'll have us down to bankruptcy. He's carried off eight of our hens already.

HENRY. Eight?

JILL. Eight of our fattest.

HENRY. Well I can't abide that. I ought to stand on till I catch that beastie myself. You'd have no fox stealing while I was about, I could promise you that . . . ! Well, you give a shout when food's on, the air has brought my appetite full up. (*He crosses out the front door.*)

JILL. I'll call in a jiff. You hurry Nellie in though. I need the logs.

HENRY. (*OFF.*) I'll hurry her. (JILL *brings a drop leaf table in from the kitchen, and two chairs. Lights down on the house. Lights up in the shed as* HENRY *steps in.* NELLIE *is sawing some logs.*)

HENRY. I didn't know you'd have to be sawing your own timber, Nellie. Where do you draw it from?

NELLIE. From the trees, where it grows.

HENRY. Do you do your own chopping them, too?

NELLIE. I do.

HENRY. Is there anything you haven't done out here?

NELLIE. Not that I could mention.

HENRY. (*Hanging the pheasants up on a nail.*) If I've upset you, Nellie, I apologize. You may think I've no manners, but that may just be a sign of my trust and good faith. If I'm to be leaving today I'd like to think I haven't left behind an enemy. Couldn't we shake on it, so I know your mind?

NELLIE. You can leave with a clear conscience, Henry. We're not enemies.

HENRY. I'd feel much firmer about it if I had your hand.

NELLIE. You have my word.

HENRY. I'd rather have your hand.

NELLIE. You don't need my hand, Henry!

HENRY. You're not afraid of me, are you?

NELLIE. No, I'm not afraid.

HENRY. Then why don't you shake? Take my hand, please.

NELLIE. Why should I?

HENRY. As a pledge.

NELLIE. Of what?

HENRY. Of us. As friends. Nellie, please.

NELLIE. Henry, stop it now. Don't be foolish!

HENRY. I'm not being foolish, Nellie! Please!

NELLIE. No!

HENRY. Why not?

NELLIE. Henry, stop!

JILL. (*Calling from the house.*) Nellie, where are you? The house is cold, and breakfast waiting!

NELLIE. I'm coming . . . ! (*She bends to pick up the logs.*)

HENRY. Let me carry that for you, Nellie.

NELLIE. Henry, stay away from me now. You've done enough . . . ! (*She grabs a few of the logs and hurries out of the shed.* HENRY *watches her go, and then picks up a knife to skin the pheasants. Lights down in the shed. Lights up in the house as* NELLIE *enters.*)

NELLIE. Why are we eating in here?

JILL. It's roomier, isn't it?

NELLIE. (*Taking the logs to fireplace.*) You mean it's prettier. It's a bigger spectacle for Henry, isn't that what you mean? I just wonder why you're rushing on so about this soldier boy, Jill. I wonder what you think is so special about him. You've never been this concerned with any boy before. What have you been thinking about him? Hm? (*She crosses into kitchen.*)

JILL. I've been thinking about you too, Nellie. I thought you might enjoy the change of view.

NELLIE. You don't have to strain yourself on my account. You've enough to do without . . .

JILL. It was no strain. I can lift a table.

NELLIE. (*Crossing in with a pan of hot coals.*) You can? That's the first I've heard about it lately . . . !

JILL. Nellie, I don't understand you today, really I don't. You've something twisting and churning around inside you, but I can't fathom it. I just like having somebody new to fuss over, you know that's the way I am. Henry's only got the one week leave, and he's just brought us in enough to fill our table four times over, and I wanted to try to return some of his thoughtfulness, that's all . . . ! Nellie, please.

NELLIE. (*Working at the fireplace.*) What?

JILL. He told me that he's had to do killing. Killing people! He looked so strange when he said it, so hurt. He said he'd trade our kind of life for what he'd had to do, anytime. It gave me a queer jump to hear him, truly it did. He's so like my brother, he's so young, Nellie. I thought a show of friendliness might help to prop him up for his trip back to Canada. He's all alone now . . . ! I'm sorry, Nellie, maybe I was just being greedy. He's company for me too, and I need that so badly now. I can't go on otherwise . . . ! (*She begins to cry.*) I'm sorry. I'll move the table back.

NELLIE. Jill, don't.

JILL. It's all right, Nellie. I'm just being silly, I know.

NELLIE. You're not being silly. It's me should be apologizing to you.

JILL. Why?

NELLIE. Because I'm letting all my dreams and my frights wash over everything we've had between us! We came out here to a creaky shop in a lonely wood and we stored it up for business, didn't we? With all the wind and the work and the war and everything else we've had to pit up against we're still running, aren't we? And we're going to keep running. If you get the chance to relax a little by fussing for Henry or anybody else, why then you do it! I won't bark at you again, I promise. You're a sweet touch of a thing, and I'm a big crusher. I've no right to spoil your kindness, so you forgive me, do you hear?

JILL. Ohh, Nellie.

NELLIE. Do you?

JILL. Of course I do.

NELLIE. Then we'll spend our days doing good deeds from now on! And whenever you catch me in a grump again, you send me to muck out the cesspool as penance. And then you can make me pump out the pond, climb for apples, and jump into the well . . . ! Aren't we two crazy birds though? Aren't we?

JILL. You are. I've always kept my sanity.

NELLIE. You won't keep it long if I make you tend to the outdoors once in a while. But you are a pretty thing when you smile, so you keep to it. One of us has to have the looks in this family . . . ! Now you rush us some breakfast, I've other things to get to.

JILL. Nellie?

NELLIE. What?

JILL. As our first good deed then, what would you think of asking Henry to stay on till his time's up? I think it'd be worth having him. If he's half the shot he was today, he could keep us in meat for the whole winter. Then we'd surely be able to keep running. Do you think you'd mind?

NELLIE. It may not suit him.

JILL. Well we can ask to find that out. But would it bother you?

NELLIE. Of course not.

JILL. Tell me if it would.

NELLIE. It wouldn't. Why should it?

JILL. Then we can do it? Shall we? Oh, I know he'll be pleased.

NELLIE. I know you will.

JILL. I know you will too, you're not fooling me. You'd like a change from my face, you know you would. But you ask him then, you're better at invitations than I am.

NELLIE. I'm no better than you.

JILL. Yes you are. You do it.

NELLIE. Why not you?

JILL. He might say no if I ask him. You do it, Nellie. Please. Please! Oh, he's coming. Ask him as soon as he's in, will you? I want to know in time for some shopping! (*She disappears into the kitchen.* HENRY *enters the kitchen, offstage.*)

HENRY. (*OFF.*) Here you are, Jill. Ready for the pot.

JILL. (*OFF.*) Thank you, Henry. Don't you go out again, though, we'll be sitting down in a jiff. You get in there and rest the meanwhile.

HENRY. (*OFF.*) Resting's for night time, isn't it?

JILL. (*OFF.*) Not for you. Now don't you go out again, you hear? Or I'll poach your eggs with mustard seed. You get in there and sit! (HENRY *enters the parlor.* NELLIE *is at the fireplace.*)

HENRY. I wish you'd let me help, Nellie. I haven't had the chance to set a proper fire since I left Canada.

NELLIE. Is that what you missed most?

HENRY. Oh I missed a lot of things.

NELLIE. Like what? Hunting?

HENRY. That.

NELLIE. Farming?

HENRY. Not much farming in Canada. Not yet, thank goodness.

NELLIE. What else?

HENRY. A good spring bed.

NELLIE. What else?

HENRY. I'm flattered you'd like to know that much about me.

NELLIE. Jill was asking what army life was about, and I couldn't tell her.

HENRY. She has a brother in service. Didn't he write?

NELLIE. He wrote from France. You came from Greece.

HENRY. Well I'll bet he didn't miss half what I did, being in France.

NELLIE. Why didn't he?

HENRY. Greece is small. There's rocky country all around. With fighting most of the time I was there. Not much chance to relax and enjoy ourselves, I can tell you that . . . ! What have you missed most being away out here? Anything special you've had to do without?

NELLIE. No.

HENRY. Nothing?

NELLIE. No.

HENRY. If only the farm'd come out right you'd have all you want, would you?

NELLIE. That's right.

HENRY. Then it's a shame the stars haven't shined properly for you.

NELLIE. Yes it is.

HENRY. I wish I could help somehow.

NELLIE. You've helped quite a lot already.

HENRY. Have I?

NELLIE. Yes you have.

HENRY. I'm very pleased to hear you say so . . . ! (JILL *enters from the kitchen with a tray of bread, margerine and jam.*)

JILL. Breadfast's on . . . ! Well now that's a pretty sight. You look right at home by the fire, Henry.

HENRY. I feel it.

JILL. I hope you'll stay then to enjoy it. Have you decided yet?

HENRY. Decided what?

NELLIE. I haven't asked him yet, Jill.

JILL. Oh shoot!

HENRY. Asked me what?

JILL. Ask him, Nellie!

HENRY. Ask me what?

NELLIE. Go on.

JILL. Ohh! If you'd consider staying on with us. Not the whole time. Not if you don't want to. Only whatever you decide. But as long as you'd like to try with us, we'd be glad to have you. It'd be no trouble, Henry, truly it wouldn't. And you've only got the few days to put up with us, so what do you say? Hm?

HENRY. What do you say, Nellie?

JILL. Nellie's said, it's your turn now.

HENRY. Ay then.

JILL. Good!

HENRY. I'd like to try forever.

JILL. I wish you had the chance . . . ! Well it's done then. Happy to have you, Henry. I only hope you like my cooking now. Sit over here and try it. I'm going to cycle into town later so we can have some fresh spreadings for dinner, and cheese. And maybe some wine. Do you like wine?

HENRY. Ay.

JILL. Then that's what we'll have with the roast pheasant I'm preparing. You'll have to do with what's left over in the meanwhile. (*She crosses back into the kitchen.*)

HENRY. I don't mind. Come to the table, Nellie. (*He holds a chair for her.*)

JILL. (*Coming in with plates.*) Well I tell you it's a

pleasure to have a gentleman in the house, truly it is . . . You sit now, Henry, I'm not finished yet. (*She returns to the kitchen.*)

HENRY. You look very handsome at the table, Nellie . . . You don't mind my being here, do you? I'd rather not stay if you do . . . Are you happy to have me?

NELLIE. You'll hear me if I'm not. (JILL *comes in with a platter of poached eggs.*)

JILL. What're you smiling about, Henry, are you comfy?

HENRY. I have two ladies to wait on me, a house to live in, a farm outside, and the woods nearby. I'll have hunting and walking and reading and talking. There's no man alive could want more. Is there?

JILL. Don't you intend to marry one day?

HENRY. Ay. If I find the right sort.

JILL. What sort would she have to be? Hm? Don't be bashful, what would she?

HENRY. Tall and strong, with a will to work and make me happy.

JILL. And how could she best do that?

HENRY. If I told you that then you'd know it all, wouldn't you Jill? And then there'd be no mystery. Such things should be a secret. Like two animals come to drink in the dark. Side by side but they don't know it. They nuzzle around with their heads in the water, and then no matter what else is about, they suddenly feel themselves close. And then they sniff. And then they test. And then they make their little noises. And then they go off together. They know when they've found what they want . . . ! (JILL's *caught* NELLIE *staring at* HENRY *and he smiles.*)

JILL. You're keen on nature, aren't you Henry?

HENRY. You have to be to live, Jill.

JILL. Not us.

HENRY. No?

JILL. We get along very well without nature, Nellie and I. You see if we don't. Your two animals in the woods'll have to be satisfied without our joining them . . . ! I'm pleased to know you can smile about it, Henry, that means we'll get along all right. (*But* HENRY *is staring at* NELLIE *again.*)

JILL. Eat now, you're forgetting your food.

HENRY. Thank you, Jill. I see what I'm doing. (*He grins at her, and then continues eating.* NELLIE *doesn't look up from her plate.* JILL *watches them both, as she tries to eat, and . . . THE LIGHTS FADE.*)

END OF ACT ONE

ACT TWO

SCENE One

Night time. The fire crackling. HENRY *is hidden in the stairwell.* JILL *returns from the kitchen to continue clearing the dinner dishes.* HENRY *suddenly leans in.*

HENRY. Hoo! (JILL *gasps.* HENRY *laughs and leaps out of the stairwell. He is clearly teasing* JILL *,and is in high good spirits. He ends up at the bookshelves.*)

JILL. What do you like most to read, Henry?

HENRY. Anything except orders.

JILL. We've got a whole stock of Captain Mayne Reid.

HENRY. Is that how you like to spend your evenings, Jill, with the Captain?

JILL. I've got lots else to read. And do, if I want. It's just that usually by the time we've finished with all the chores that have got to be done —

HENRY. What then?

JILL. Well the days are short and the nights are long so we usually pick a sitting job to keep us till bedtime. I do anyway. I write letters and I play the harp . . .

HENRY. Do you?

JILL. Yes, and I sew, and . . .

HENRY. Do you play well?

JILL. Not so bad you'd have to leave the room.

HENRY. Do you mean your hens never squawk while you're at it?

JILL. Our hens squawk at anything, you've seen that.

HENRY. They were tame enough today, weren't they?

JILL. Yes they were.

HENRY. And laid a basketfull, didn't they?

JILL. I don't know what you fed them but they surely did.

HENRY. I fed them what they've always had, but I told them something, too.

JILL. What?

HENRY. That I'd have their necks the next yap out of them! Especially that big white leghorn with the brown marking. There's the yappiest thing I've ever heard in a yard!

JILL. That's Patty. She's Nellie's bird.

HENRY. Is she?

JILL. She won't touch her food unless Nellie holds it out for her.

HENRY. Won't she though?

JILL. Nellie'd no sooner lop away at her than she would me.

HENRY. Then I'm liable to have the both of you before I'm done. If you turn out to be a squawker, too . . . ! (*He follows her as she crosses to the kitchen.*)

JILL. Henry, stay here.

HENRY. Come play the harp for me first.

JILL. Henry.

HENRY. You cooked a marvelous dinner, and you stuffed me full, and now you've got to help me work it off.

JILL. Nellie's alone in there.

HENRY. I'm alone here.

JILL. She's put in a hard day today.

HENRY. Haven't I?

JILL. You have, but we didn't ask you to.

HENRY. And now all I'm asking you to do is lead me to the harp . . .

JILL. Henry . . .

HENRY. And play while I sing. I've got to clear my lungs somehow!

JILL. Clear them of what?

HENRY. Of happiness! I'm so full of good spirits, I'm liable to pop away into the woods and dance the night to Islington!

JILL. Well dance then, I have to help Nellie . . . ! (*She crosses into the kitchen.* HENRY *stares after her for a moment. Sound of a dog barking.* HENRY *opens the front door and stands looking out.* NELLIE *comes hurriedly into the room,* JILL *a distance behind her.*)

NELLIE. You'll blow out the fire, Henry.

HENRY. There's no breeze tonight, Nellie. Even the sky is still.

JILL. But cold!

HENRY. Ay. (*He closes the door.*) You finished without Jill's help, I see.

NELLIE. I always do.

JILL. The washing. I have to pile the things for her.

HENRY. Have you finished piling them now?

JILL. What's left'll dry 'till morning.

HENRY. Well who's for a walk in the woods, then? We can take the gun and stock up for the morning.

JILL. You must be dizzy Henry. Now's no time to be tramping about out there. (NELLIE *crosses to the blanket chest for her needlework.*)

HENRY. Now's the best time, Jill. When all the rest of the world's away indoors. When all the busybodies are shut up tight and you can walk free, without interruption . . . ! You come with me, Nellie. Will you? You're not afraid of a little night air, are you?

NELLIE. No.

JILL. She's afraid she may have to use her legs tomorrow and they'd be all wearied out.

HENRY. That's a small reason.

JILL. Big enough for us.

NELLIE. Thank you, Henry. I think I'd rather stick to my needling tonight.

HENRY. Is that your last word?

NELLIE. Yes it is.

HENRY. Then that's how we shall have to leave it. I don't want to make myself a pest . . . !

JILL. Is walking in the woods what you were most fond of in the evenings, Henry?

HENRY. Ay. Looking out for rabbits, and trying to scare up a deer or two.

JILL. We heard you used to scare up all the neighbors.

HENRY. Where did you hear that?

JILL. In the village. This afternoon, when I cycled in.

HENRY. What did they tell you?

JILL. Mostly there were just a lot of dark looks and shaking of heads when I mentioned your name.

HENRY. There were, were there?

JILL. And they talked about you not being the greatest milker in the world.

NELLIE. Jill.

HENRY. Did they?

JILL. And about your loafing off the work and chasing your rabbits and jollywogging all day while your grand dad tended the farm.

HENRY. Who told you all that? What were their names?

JILL. They're none to get fierce about, Henry.

HENRY. Now I've reached my size I can get fierce about any of them. That's what's needed!

JILL. Why?

NELLIE. They're small-minded people, Henry.

HENRY. I know what they are. And I know what they say! Are they friends of yours, these loud mouths?

NELLIE. We try never to meet them, but we have to on shop days.

HENRY. Ay, that's it. That's all they're good for is their bloody shop days! They're the kind that never care if the stars burn, or the world spins, or a mountain moves. They're tiny, tiny people, crowding the earth for no good reason except to squeeze off anybody that interferes with their shop days!

NELLIE. You sound as though you've had some run-ins with them. Have you?

HENRY. Run-ins enough.

JILL. What kind?

HENRY. I've had to bend to a switch for skipping through a street because of them!

NELLIE. What?

HENRY. My grand dad used to whip me on anyone's complaint, and they all had something to say about how and why a strip like me shouldn't be crossing their property, or fishing their streams, or passing their stores in the middle of a day. That's what they complained about! They couldn't stand to see me roaming the land while they sat fast thinking about their linens, and their gardens, and their next day's business! (NELLIE *laughs*.) They couldn't stand to see me laughing at them for the poor frightened things that they are. Life is a run, and they're afraid to move! Life is a wind, and they sit huddled in their houses, hugging their belongings, and sucking their thumbs! They live in green houses, that's what they do, only they grow weeds in their minds instead of ideas. It's their only claim to ever being thought of again . . . ! (*Sound of dogs barking in the distance.* HENRY *rushes to the door to look again.*)

JILL. They were up last night too.

HENRY. I heard them. They're after something big, that's for sure.

NELLIE. What do you think it is?

HENRY. Maybe that fox you've been talking about . . . ! Can I have your gun Nellie? I want to try to bring him down. (*He rushes to the kitchen for the rifle.*)

JILL. No!

HENRY. Why not? Can't I, Nellie? You won't worry about me, will you?

JILL. We'll worry about the neighbors with you shooting in the dark.

HENRY. I haven't hit a neighbor yet, Jill. Not with years of trying. Let me take the gun, please Nellie! Please!

NELLIE. You'll have to look out for the dogs.

HENRY. I won't take a dog for a fox.

NELLIE. But they might mistake you . . . ! We'll only be up an hour, after that we'll be in bed.

HENRY. If I catch him then I'll wake you to celebrate. (*He races to the kitchen for the gun.*) Thank you Nellie. (*He quickly crosses out.*)

JILL. I don't like that, Nellie. They told me he was always hopping about with a gun.

NELLIE. So?

JILL. Don't let him have it when he asks.

NELLIE. How shall I stop him? We let him hunt for us in the daylight. Shall we stop him in the morning, too?

JILL. It's the way he looks about it, I don't like.

NELLIE. How?

JILL. So excited. So intense!

NELLIE. He's a young boy. He has to carry on a bit or he won't be comfortable.

JILL. Then I won't be comfortable.

NELLIE. Oh you're silly. You wanted to help his loneliness, didn't you? Well he's out there now, tracking the woods, just as unlonely as he can be.

JILL. I don't like his temper, Nellie. And I don't like the way he's been carrying on in here either. Asking you to walk, and asking me to play. We're going to have to keep an eye on him, you see if we don't.

NELLIE. What, are you afraid he'll steal some of our chickens?

JILL. No. I'm afraid . . . (*She stops.*)

NELLIE. What? What are you afraid of?

JILL. I know what I'm talking about Nellie, and if you don't then it's because . . . never mind.

NELLIE. What?

JILL. Never mind.

NELLIE. Tell me.

JILL. Never mind, Nellie. Never mind . . . ! (*She puts out the candles on the fireplace mantel, and . . .*)

THE LIGHTS FADE

SCENE TWO

JILL *still in front of the fire.* NELLIE *is now standing against the staircase wall.*

JILL. Well I can't wait anymore. It's been hours since

last the dogs barked . . . ! You've put two extra logs on the fire already. Are you going to stay the night?

NELLIE. No.

JILL. Till when then?

NELLIE. I haven't tired yet.

JILL. Won't you come up with me anyway? Nellie?

NELLIE. I'll settle you in, but I won't sleep. I can't.

JILL. Why not?

NELLIE. No reason.

JILL. Will you come back down?

NELLIE. Yes, I think so. Why?

JILL. Then I won't go.

NELLIE. Why won't you?

JILL. I don't like to sleep without you there, you know that.

NELLIE. One of these days you'll have to. Forever.

JILL. What do you mean?

NELLIE. When I'm dead.

JILL. I'll go long before you, no fear of that.

NELLIE. Do you know what you are, Jill? You're a faker. With all your aches and all your ailments, you've got a heart that'll beat on 'till doomsday. You're a sham, that's what you are . . . ! Look now if you're really buttered out and you can't even blink your eyes open enough to sit and talk, then I'll set you in your room, fill your bottle, and hum you off to dreamland. All right?

JILL. Are you waiting up for Henry?

NELLIE. Of course not.

JILL. I think you are, Nellie.

NELLIE. I've just told you I'm not.

JILL. If you were, why would you be?

NELLIE. Jill, I'm not. Don't be silly.

JILL. I've seen the way he looks at you, and I've seen the way you look at him.

NELLIE. How?

JILL. It's no good your pretending surprise. I see what I see . . .

NELLIE. You can't see anything with your eyes.

JILL. And I know what I know!

NELLIE. And I'm asking, what?

JILL. You're thinking about going away with him!

NELLIE. Jill, have you gone off your chump?

JILL. I wanted him to stay on because I thought he'd be a bit of fun in the house, but he's begun stamping about the place as if he's half-owner and he's been looking you up and down like a farmer checking stock at a fair.

NELLIE. Jill!

JILL. If you haven't seen him then I have! He moves to you like a stable hand with a new horse! We came out here to get away from looks like that, didn't we? Didn't we?

NELLIE. Yes, we did.

JILL. So if Henry's going to start fiddling around with that same kind of look then we'll have to get away from him too, won't we?

NELLIE. Jill—

JILL. Well I think he's already started! He's not just a boy, Nellie, he's a grown man. He's got a gun in his hands and ideas in his head, and he's not just the sweet thing we imagined. He's got a temper and he's got a reputation for trouble.

NELLIE. Whatever trouble he's caused . . .

JILL. I'm not talking about his loafing off the work— although we have yet to see how long he's going to give us a hand!

NELLIE. Jill, will you hush now?

JILL. I'm talking about his prowling through the

woods! They told me he was out there every night. Every night, Nellie. Warm or cold. Light or dark!

NELLIE. He was fifteen that time.

JILL. But he's got that same kind of look about him now! Whenever he mentions the woods, or animals, or the gun, he's got an excitement inside him that shines through like a beacon. You must be dumb if you can't see that!

NELLIE. Are you frightened of him Jill? Is that what it is?

JILL. Yes!

NELLIE. Well I'm not!

JILL. I know you aren't, that's what I'm arguing about . . . !

NELLIE. Listen now . . .

JILL. Ohh, Nellie—

NELLIE. Listen! We've asked him on, and he's said yes, and he's done nothing yet that I can call a real bother, and if he's got some great need to be off in the woods while the rest of us sit by our fires then more power to him. He's a bigger man for it than we are.

JILL. Why?

NELLIE. The woods aren't the safest place you could name, are they? A gun isn't an easy thing to handle well, is it? Henry was right when he said that those gossipers were jealous of him. They're jealous of us too. Because we're doing what none of them thought we could do alone, and we're doing what they hoped we wouldn't be able to do because that'd prove that we were better than they are! And if you're frightened of Henry then it's for the same reason. You think he's better than you, braver than you. And he is! He can't cook, but he can provide. He can't hang curtains, but he can sturdy a barn. He can't sit, but he can run . . . ! Jill, I'm not angry at you, and I'm not trying to slight you. If you're tired now, please let me put you to bed. I won't be long to follow. I promise. Please. Please!

JILL. All right.

NELLIE. I'll heat your bottle now, while you ready up.

JILL. Nellie!

NELLIE. What?

JILL. You won't leave me though, will you? Will you?

NELLIE. Leaving you would be like leaving half my life, how could I do that? Go on up, Jill. Go on. (JILL *crosses to the stairs with the lamp. Suddenly there is the sound of chickens screeching in the near distance.*)

JILL. It's the fox! (*A gunshot roars out close by.*)

HENRY. (*OFF.*) Come look what I've caught you, Nellie!

JILL. (*She flings the door open.*) Is that you, Henry?

HENRY. (*OFF.*) Ay. Come see what I've got for you! (NELLIE *crosses for her coat.*)

JILL. Don't go out there now.

NELLIE. Why not?

JILL. Henry, you come in here now, and put the gun away!

HENRY. (*OFF.*) I've caught your chicken thief, Jill!

JILL. You come in here now, never mind what you caught us!

NELLIE. Stop your yelling, Jill.

JILL. Don't go out there, Nellie. I don't trust what he's up to. It's too cold out.

NELLIE. Jill, let me pass.

JILL. I don't want you to leave me, Nellie! Please! Please!

HENRY. (*OFF.*) Step back into the light and I'll show you what a beauty he is, Jill. (JILL *moves back as* HENRY *enters holding a dead fox.*) He'll make you a fine fur piece, won't he? Is he the one's been haunting you all this while, Nellie?

JILL. Is he, Nellie?

NELLIE. I'd swear he is.

HENRY. Then you won't be losing any more chicks or sleep, will you?

JILL. Thank you, Henry, but take him out of here now. We don't want a dirty beast in our parlor.

HENRY. He isn't dirty, Jill. I've shaken most of the blood out of him.

JILL. Take him out of here, Henry! Get him out!

HENRY. You want to come watch me peg him up, Nellie?

JILL. No she doesn't!

HENRY. I wasn't asking you, Jill.

JILL. Nellie has to fill my bottle.

HENRY. Does she?

JILL. And then we're going to sleep.

HENRY. Are you?

JILL. Tell him, Nellie.

HENRY. Do you want to go to bed, or do you want to come with me now, Nellie?

NELLIE. You go on up, Jill. I'll be back soon.

HENRY. I'll fetch your bottle for you myself. Go on up, Jill. I won't keep her long . . . ! (*He takes the lamp, opens the door for* NELLIE, *and they step out. Lights down in the house. Lights up in the shed as* HENRY *and* NELLIE *enter.*)

HENRY. He is real beauty, isn't he? I almost hated to bring him down. The farms and the farmers, and the shops and the shopkeepers have been crowding his territory just as they've been crowding mine. We're both creatures of the wood, you know. You feel a little sorry for him now, do you? Mind you don't catch his fleas. (NELLIE'*s been stroking the animal's fur, but she doesn't stop.*) Have you never felt a fox before?

NELLIE. No.

HENRY. There's enough electricity in that tail to light up a whole house if you could gather it . . . Are you fond of electricity?

NELLIE. Where did you catch him, at the coop?

HENRY. Ay. He came in under the gate, just as I knew he would. I let him have a couple of sniffs, and then I gave him the blast. I was waiting for him.

NELLIE. How did you know that's the way he'd come?

HENRY. I felt it.

NELLIE. And how did you do that?

HENRY. I willed it . . . ! I'll tell you something, Nellie. A hunter if he's a real hunter, never just walks into a forest and says to an animal, "please fall to my gun beastie." It's a slower, subtler thing than that. When you hunt you have to gather yourself to bring down what you're out for. You have to coil everything you are, just as a snake does when he's about to strike, and then you have to focus not just your eyes but your whole mind and soul on the thing you're after, so it becomes like a fate. Your will against his. And then when you reach your true pitch, and you finally come into range, you don't aim as you would at a bottle, or a can of chowder. It's your will that carries the bullet through. It's your will that brings the creature down. It has to be the will or you'll never win. It's whoever's will is the weakest that's the loser . . . ! Have you never hunted that way?

NELLIE. No, I haven't.

HENRY. That's why you're so far behind . . . ! Well, if Jill won't have him, shall I make a fur piece for you?

NELLIE. No, thank you.

HENRY. Why not?

NELLIE. I never wear fur.

HENRY. Why not, if you like the feel of it?

NELLIE. I don't like the feel of it.

HENRY. You did just now.

NELLIE. That wasn't liking.

HENRY. What was it?

NELLIE. I was interested, that's all.

HENRY. Take him, Nellie. I want you to have him.

NELLIE. He's yours, you caught him.

HENRY. I'd like to give him to you.

NELLIE. Why should you?

HENRY. Because I want to.

NELLIE. Why do you?

HENRY. Come here, and I'll tell you. Come close, Nellie, so I can say it. (JILL *suddenly calls from the house.*)

JILL. (*OFF.*) Nellie.

NELLIE. I've got to go in now.

HENRY. No you don't.

NELLIE. Jill's calling me, can't you hear?

HENRY. But she can fill her own bottle, can't she?

NELLIE. She can, but she likes me to do it.

HENRY. What else does she like you to do? Tuck her in, and whisper in her ear that she's safe and sound for the night?

NELLIE. That's right.   .

HENRY. That's a wastey habit, isn't it? The more you whisper, the more she'll want you to, and soon you'll be spending half your evenings tucking her in and filling her bottle. Is that what you want for yourself, Nellie? Is that the way you want to spend the rest of your life? You ought to be thinking about more worthwhile things!

NELLIE. Such as what?

JILL. (*OFF.*) Nellie!

HENRY. Such as marrying, and helping tuck in a man! Have you never though about that?

NELLIE. Yes, I've thought about it.

HENRY. But running away out here, you must've thought everything wrong!

JILL. (*OFF.*) Nellie, where are you?

NELLIE. I'm coming . . . !

HENRY. Let her call, it won't hurt.

NELLIE. Henry, let me pass.

HENRY. I have some needs and likes too, Nellie.

NELLIE. Henry.

HENRY. There's been no thought of my marrying anybody till now, but you're what nobody else has ever been!

JILL. Nellie!

NELLIE. Henry, please!

HENRY. You speak your mind, and you manage a farm, but you breathe warm, and you think warm, I know you do!

NELLIE. Henry.

HENRY. That's what a woman ought to do.

JILL. (*OFF.*) Nellie?

HENRY. Not like Jill. She's a little flower, that's what she is, and she'll wilt fast, take my word.

NELLIE. Henry, please.

HENRY. I want you to think about marrying me. I want you to!

JILL. (*OFF.*) Nellie: Answer me!

HENRY. Think about me now, Nellie, never mind her! Will you? Will you?

NELLIE. Will I what?

HENRY. Think about me . . .

JILL. (*OFF.*)Nellieeeee . . . !

HENRY. Think about marrying me. Me, Nellie, me!

JILL. Nellie! Nellie . . . !

HENRY. Think about marrying me. Will you?

NELLIE. Yes. Yes!

JILL. (*OFF.*)Nellie! Nellie, Nellie . . . !

HENRY. Think about me!

NELLIE. Yes, yes, yes, yes, yes . . . ! (*She rushes out.*)

JILL. (*OFF.*) Nellie! Nellie! Nellie! (*Lights down on the shed. Lights up in the house. Jill stands in the doorway screaming.*) Nellie! Nellie! Nellie!

NELLIE. (*OFF.*)I'm here. I'm here. (*In a moment she appears, and steps into the house.*)

JILL. What were you doing out there? Why didn't you come when I called?

NELLIE. I did.

JILL. I called a dozen times before you got here.

NELLIE. I didn't hear you then.

JILL. You're lying, Nellie.

NELLIE. Don't say that to me!

JILL. You are. I know you are . . . !

NELLIE. I'll get you your bottle now. (*She crosses into the kitchen.*)

JILL. What did Henry say to you? What did he try to do?

NELLIE. Nothing.

JILL. He did, he did, Nellie. Tell me!

NELLIE. Silly boy. He's got himself so excited over the hunting he's done, he's out to prove he can catch me, too. He asked me to marry him, that was all. (*She crosses in with a kettle for the fire.*)

JILL. Did you tell him to leave?

NELLIE. No.

JILL. Why didn't you?

NELLIE. Because he's a foolish boy, that's why! I'd no sooner think of marring him than I would our horse in the barn! Now shush about it!

JILL. Nellie, I think he ought to leave. Why should we have him stay now?

NELLIE. He can fill our table, that's what you said.

JILL. You're making us foolish, Nellie. You're letting him take advantage of us!

NELLIE. We'll be taking advantage of him.

JILL. No we won't. That's what I thought, but I see now he stands to gain more than we do. Much more!

NELLIE. What?

JILL. You! And me! He wants this place, Nellie, and he wants us to work it for him! He wants me for his kitchen and you for his bed!

NELLIE. Jill!

JILL. And he wants the farm for his future! He has nothing in Canada, he told us that. He lived wild, on the side of a mountain.

NELLIE. Will you stop now?

JILL. He's got to go, Nellie. Tell him.

NELLIE. You go on upstairs now . . .

JILL. Why won't you listen to me? I'm telling you . . . (*There is a knock at the door.*)

NELLIE. Come in. (HENRY *enters.*)

HENRY. Not in bed yet, Jill?

NELLIE. She will be soon.

HENRY. You weren't waiting for me, were you . . . ? (JILL *takes the lamp, glares at* HENRY, *and mounts the stairs.*) That was a fishy look. What's got into her?

NELLIE. You asked me to think about you Henry. Well I have. I don't appreciate your tomfoolery in the shed just now, and if you're to stay on here you must promise never to do or say anything like that again. I have to ask that condition, or I'll have to ask you to leave . . . ! Now which is it going to be?

HENRY. Whichever you'd rather, Nellie.

NELLIE. It's up to you to decide.

HENRY. I think it's up to you.

NELLIE. It's your choice, Henry, not mine . . . ! (*She puts her needlework in the blanket chest.*)

HENRY. You call what I said in the shed, tomfoolery?

NELLIE. I do. I certainly do.

HENRY. That means you don't think I was serious.

NELLIE. I can't see how you could be. You've only been here but one day, you've been a soldier for three years, you feel you've been lonely, so you ask me to marry you. Well if that isn't tomfoolery, what is? I'm very flattered, but I can't think you'll still be serious in the morning, really I can't.

HENRY. Laughing at me is no way out, Nellie.

NELLIE. Out of what?

HENRY. Out of answering my question. When I'm serious I don't like to be taken lightly. If what I said was so much tomfoolery, then why must I promise never to do it again? It hasn't hurt you, has it?

NELLIE. It certainly hasn't.

HENRY. But you're afraid it might.

NELLIE. No I'm not.

HENRY. Then why must I promise never . . .

NELLIE. We've no time here for fooling, Henry! Jill and I have much too much to do without bothering about you and your fancies!

HENRY. I haven't bothered Jill, have I? I thought . . .

NELLIE. You certainly have!

HENRY. How?

NELLIE. Never mind how, Henry, that's my business! (*She crosses to the fireplace for the kettle of water.*)

HENRY. You seem very concerned about Jill.

NELLIE. I am.

HENRY. Even more than you are about yourself. Is it because of her you're asking me to stop saying what I did outside?

NELLIE. No it isn't.

HENRY. Is it?

NELLIE. I told you no, Henry!

HENRY. But I don't think you mean no . . . !

NELLIE. It's time for me to be upstairs.

HENRY. Nellie . . . ! I am serious about you. I may stop asking it, but I won't stop thinking it.

NELLIE. You can stay, Henry. But only on condition . . . ! (*She crosses to the stairs and THE LIGHTS FADE.*)

END OF ACT TWO

ACT THREE

Scene One

The house is empty. Sound of chopping outside. The time is afternoon. The chopping suddenly stops.

NELLIE. (*Off.*) Jill, don't come over the fence. Wait now.

JILL. (*OFF.*) I'm all right.

NELLIE. (*OFF.*) You'll dump all those packages. Wait 'till I get there . . . ! You crazy thing, why are you coming this way? Where's the cycle?

JILL. (*OFF.*) I twisted a spoke coming into the crossing. I had to leave it with the Manders.

NELLIE. (*OFF.*) You know you balance isn't always right. Why do you have to tempt the fates?

JILL. (*OFF.*) The fence is no higher than the bike, and you let me ride that alone.

NELLIE. (*OFF.*) You've had practice on the bike! When are you going to pick it up again? (*JILL appears first with several parcels. NELLIE carries several more.*)

JILL. Tomorrow, or the day after. There's no hurry about it, is there? (*Crossing into the kitchen.*)

NELLIE. Henry asked to borrow it this afternoon. (*She crosses in after JILL.*)

JILL. Did he? Why?

NELLIE. I think he wanted a tour of the town for a change.

JILL. (*Crossing into parlor where she removes her gloves, hat and scarf.*) Three days of farm work is a lit-

55

tle too much for him, is it? He can walk in if he's that eager . . . !

NELLIE. It isn't only the work, Jill. It's us too, I'm sure.

JILL. How is that? Hm?

NELLIE. He knows we haven't taken too easily to his staying on. You pick at him every chance you get and I . . .

JILL. I do not. Does he say I do?

NELLIE. He wouldn't say it out . . .

JILL. Oh wouldn't he?

NELLIE. But he's no blinder to us than we are to him. We sit, mouth tight, every evening, and bury ourselves in whatever we've got, while he's left to diddle about in our books, or . . .

JILL. Or stretch into the woods for an hour's prowl!

NELLIE. (*Appearing in kitchen doorway munching a piece of bread.*) Well we're not helping him keep out, are we? If that's what bothers you most then why don't you leave off flailing about his manners at the table, and the mud on his boots . . .

JILL. If he was anybody else you'd flail about the same things, you know you would! (*She crosses into the kitchen and reappears again with a container to refill the kerosene lamp.*)

NELLIE. You said you were going to try to prop him up for his trip back to Canada, didn't you?

JILL. Oh, it doesn't matter a damn to Henry whether I mind his manners or not. He still gets his special consideration from you anyway, doesn't he?

NELLIE. What special consideration?

JILL. Who lays out his blanket in the morning and makes his bed? I don't.

NELLIE. He doesn't either, that's why . . .

JILL. And who's after him now for tea, or for cookies, or to rest himself after every half-hour's work?

NELLIE. As long as he's here, I can see no point in being rude to him, Jill.

JILL. It's not rudeness! I'm just trying to get him to remember that this is our house, and our farm . . .

NELLIE. He knows that.

JILL. Well I tell you truly, Nellie, it makes me a little sick to see him flopped out in our parlor with his legs lapping up half our room and his dirty boots on the floor and . . .

NELLIE. He cleans his boots as often as I . . .

JILL. . . . his jacket off, looking to every move we make, like a hawk on the wing! He's too hot, Nellie. He's burning up with a need to make something happen. And if we don't put a damper on him soon he's going to break loose and I don't know what!

NELLIE. What? (*The door suddenly opens and* HENRY *enters, with the gun.*)

JILL. Ah-hah!

HENRY. I'm sorry, Jill, did I surprise you?

JILL. You really don't care a damn about manners, do you Henry? Well what is it now? What do you want?

HENRY. I saw you coming across the field and I called but you didn't answer. I wanted to help you with your load.

JILL. You might've helped Nellie with her chopping if helping was so much on your mind.

NELLIE. I wouldn't have let him.

HENRY. Nellie never lets me help her, you know that.

JILL. Perhaps that's because you don't ask hard enough . . . ! (*She crosses into kitchen with the empty kerosene container.*)

NELLIE. Jill slept on a rock last night, Henry. It's put a

lump in her equilibrium . . . Did you have any luck in the woods?

HENRY. I wasn't out long enought. I only picked up the gun a few minutes ago. I came to ask Jill what's become of the bike. I noticed . . .

NELLIE. She's had a wheel twisted.

JILL. (*Bringing in a package to put in the sideboard.*) It was only a spoke.

NELLIE. It put the whole thing out though. She'll try to pick it up tomorrow, for fixing.

JILL. So you'll have to spend your afternoon in the forest again, Henry. There's no way out of it!

HENRY. There isn't much else I can do, is there? We've settled all the feeding and tidying up.

NELLIE. You go on, Henry. You're not here to slave away on our work.

JILL. Yes go on, Henry. We can get along very nicely without you!

HENRY. Nellie, how would you like to come with me this time? So I can give you some lessons for after I'm gone. You haven't been out there in a while. You're liable to lose your way. Do you want to come with me?

NELLIE. Another time, Henry.

HENRY. Another time and I may not be here.

JILL. Then we'll just have to manage without you, won't we?

HENRY. Yes, you will. Come on out, Nellie. I promise you won't regret it. I'll show you the rabbit hideouts, and the deer paths . . .

NELLIE. Not now Henry, I have a job to finish.

HENRY. Damn the job. Come with me, Nellie!

NELLIE. I can't . . . ! (*And she crosses out.* HENRY *stacks the rifle just behind the front door.*)

JILL. If you're disappointed, Henry, well, that's too bad . . . ! (*She begins sweeping out the room.*)

HENRY. You don't like me here now, do you Jill? Why not?

JILL. Don't weasel about it, Henry, that doesn't become you.

HENRY. What have I done to you? Tell me.

JILL. You know as well as I what you've been trying to do. Not to me, to everybody and everything.

HENRY. What?

JILL. Ohh —

HENRY. What?

JILL. Nellie told me you asked her to marry you.

HENRY. I knew she would, and yes I did.

JILL. Well why did you? You're not in love with her. Why then?

HENRY. What makes you think I don't love her? (*Sound of chopping offstage.*)

JILL. I know you don't. You couldn't.

HENRY. Why couldn't I?

JILL. Oh stop it, Henry, you haven't got the talent to play the game without our seeing through you. You're a fortune hunter, that's all you are, and we know it now truly we do.

HENRY. What great fortune do you think . . .

JILL. But let me tell you this . . . even if Nellie should find you attractive, and even if you were clever enough to charm her into marriage, I'd never let you stay on here! Never. You'd have to take her to Canada and keep her tied to you so she wouldn't slip off the mountain you live on while you were asleep! Whatever happens, Sunday you're leaving this farm, and you won't ever be welcome to return, not as long as I have anything to say about it . . . !

HENRY. I'm glad we've got it straight now, Jill.

JILL. I'm happy you're so pleased. Now will you move out of here so I can work?

HENRY. But if you're that frightened of me . . .

JILL. I'm not frightened of you.

HENRY. . . . then why don't you have me leave sooner? Won't Nellie let you?

JILL. We're not rude, Henry.

HENRY. It wouldn't be rudeness.

JILL. We don't like to take advantage of someone wandering about.

HENRY. It's your house, and your property.

JILL. You have nowhere else to go!

HENRY. I can go a thousand places! Do you think this is my last chance for a bed in this world?

JILL. Don't shout, Henry!

HENRY. Now let me tell you something, little miss! You're scared to death, that's what you are. You're afraid I'm going to grab Nellie away from you, and then you'll be all alone to face the fierceness of the life around you. Your bones chatter and your stomach spins just thinking about it! Well, if you can get Nellie to ask me off his place anytime before Sunday I'll go, and you won't hear a mumble out of me for it. But if you can't get her to do that, then we'll know who means the most here, and there won't be anymore fuss or palaver about that! Now you stick to your kitchen and your cupboards, and I'll soon have the problem nubbed down for you! (*He hurries out of the house.* JILL *watches him go, and then decides to follow him. Lights down in the house.*)

HENRY. (*Calling.*) Nellie! Come here! (*The chopping stops.*) Come here, Nellie.

NELLIE. What is it?

HENRY. Come here . . . ! (*He crosses into the woodshed.* NELLIE *appears.*) You wanted to walk out into the woods with me just before, didn't you? You would have liked peeking in at birds' nests and rabbit holes with me beside you, wouldn't you? Wouldn't you?

NELLIE. What makes you think that?

HENRY. What's holding you in, Nellie, say what's on your mind! I've told you what ticks inside of me. I've trusted you with whatever good or bad might come of it. The least you can do is be honest with me now . . . ! I've just had a to-do with Jill. She says no matter what, she'll never let you marry me. "She" never will! I can't abide that, Nellie. I've asked you to marry me from the heart, and that's the deepest there is of me. If it's really no, it's got to be you that says it. I'm not fooling now, Nellie, you see I'm not. So tell me, why can't you marry me? Why won't you? You don't love anybody else, do you? Do you?

NELLIE. No.

HENRY. Not even Jill, do you?

NELLIE. That's something different.

HENRY. But it isn't love! Tell me the truth now, can you picture yourself growing old and white with no one but Jill beside you? Is that a painting you'd like to hang in your room? Couldn't you rather think of we two together, holding hands in the snow, still tracking the wild parts of the earth? Feeling cold and fire, and wet, and hot, feeling the two of us standing high and alive, while the dullards sit safe in their houses? I could get a job if I had to, I'm not a waster, Nellie. I've saved half what they paid me the last three years, and I won't mind using it to give us a start anywhere! I want you to marry me, Nellie. What's wrong about it? Say you will. Say you will.

NELLIE. No!

HENRY. You want the feel of me. You need it! Say you'll have me, Nellie. Say it!

NELLIE. No!

HENRY. You will, Nellie. I swear you will!

NELLIE. No!

HENRY. Yes.

NELLIE. No.

HENRY. Yes!

NELLIE. No! (HENRY *grabs her and kisses her.* NELLIE *clutches tightly to him.* JILL *suddenly appears in the doorway.*)

JILL. Nellie! Have you lost your mind?

HENRY. (*Pulling away from* NELLIE, *smiling.*) She hasn't lost her mind, Jill. She's just decided to have me.

JILL. No!

HENRY. Look at her, Nellie. Tell her you've agreed to marry me.

NELLIE. It's true, Jill.

JILL. No!

HENRY. It's true, Jill.

JILL. No, no, no, no, it's impossible!

HENRY. Mustn't snap, Jill.

JILL. I won't let you do it. Look at me. Look at me, Nellie! Are you bewitched?

HENRY. She isn't bewitched. Just happy. (*He draws* JILL *away.*)

JILL. Take your hands off me!

HENRY. Leave us alone now, Jill.

JILL. You leave us alone!

HENRY. Get away, I said.

JILL. Nellie, look at me. Look at me, please!

HENRY. Get away, Jill . . . ! (*He pushes her away. She suddenly shrieks, and runs to the house.*)

NELLIE. Jill, wait! (*She tries to follow, but* HENRY *stops her.*)

HENRY. Your place is with me now.

NELLIE. Henry, let me be

HENRY. You've pledged yourself.

NELLIE. I pledged myself to Jill a long time ago.

HENRY. Your place is with me now!

NELLIE. I've broken her heart. I have to go to her!

HENRY. You have to stay with me, or you'll break my heart!

NELLIE. Yours?

HENRY. Do you think I haven't got one? You think my heart can't feel what hers does? Feel it! Feel it . . . ! (*He holds her hand to his chest, and she slowly subsides.*) I want you with me, Nellie. Jill is only crying. She won't hurt herself . . . ! Now give me you hand. I want you to marry me before I go. Do you hear? What is it?

NELLIE. (*Crying.*) Henry, why me? You could so easily find someone who'd suit you better. You know you could.

HENRY. How could I do that?

NELLIE. You're young. You must've fooled with girls before. You've only been back this little while, how do you know I'm what you want? I'm almost thirty.

HENRY. What has age to do with it?

NELLIE. I've settled here. I'm happy here.

HENRY. You know you're not.

NELLIE. You can't count on me, Henry. I fly up and down like a gull. I don't know what moves me, and I don't know what'll keep me still!

HENRY. I will!

NELLIE. How can you be so sure?

HENRY. I will, Nellie. You know I will . . . ! Now wipe your mind of what's been before and think of the future. You can't let Jill, and you can't let the farm, and you can't let anything cloud that sight! Yes, I've fooled with girls before, but when I marry I want to feel it's for all my life, and when I think of all my life, and of you, then the two go together . . . ! I know what I want, Nellie, and the only thing that'll satisfy me is you. So you'll have me, won't you? Won't you?

NELLIE. We can't marry before you leave. Even if we stick up the banns in the morning there won't be time enough.

HENRY. I'll come back then.

NELLIE. From Canada?

HENRY. From camp. I'm not to be shipped for another month. I'll leave here a day early so they'll still owe me one, and then I'll fix a time to claim it . . . You can't refuse me, Nellie, you know you can't. You know you can't . . . ! (*He kisses her again, even more voluptuously, and . . .*)

THE LIGHTS FADE

SCENE TWO

Evening. The wind is full again. JILL *is laying out the dinner things.* HENRY *comes in with a load of wood for the fire.*

HENRY. Nellie not down yet?

JILL. You don't see her, do you?

HENRY. Nellie, dinner's waiting . . . ! Jill, you're not going to grudge me for all this, are you? What has to be, will. But I want you to know I'll always remember how fine you've been to Nellie, and to me, and if one day you ever feel the urge to try your luck in Canada, why we'll stake you to a bed, your meals, and even a couple of lumberjack friends. England is drying up now, take my word. There's no juice left in her beams. You'll be wasting your years trying to live full in a land full of shopkeepers.

JILL. Thank you, Henry. It's nice of you to seem so concerned.

HENRY. I am.

JILL. If I didn't know what a thief you are, I'd almost believe you. Nellie, I'm ready to pour! (*And* JILL *crosses into the kitchen.*)

NELLIE. (*OFF.*) I'm coming . . . !

HENRY. I'm sorry you won't be reconciled with me, Jill. I'd appreciate your friendship . . . ! (JILL *returns with a tureen of soup.*) I know you and Nellie haven't made any selling plans yet. If there's anything I can do to help you there, I'd like to. I might know some fellows who'd want to buy the place. You're not going to try to keep it up alone, are you? Are you going to look for another partner, is that the idea . . . ? What are you gawking at? Have I said anything strange?

JILL. Who did you have in mind to buy the farm?

HENRY. No one for sure, but I'll certainly ask about it when I get back to camp.

JILL. You'd buy it yourself if it was cheap enough, wouldn't you? Wouldn't you?

HENRY. Why would I?

JILL. You want this place, don't you Henry? It's all over your face. It's been all over your face since you came. Well you won't get it, not from me.

HENRY. I don't want it from you, Jill.

JILL. You want it with me, to service it for you. Well you can't have either, Henry. You've got Nellie, but that's all!

HENRY. That's all I'm looking for.

JILL. Is it?

HENRY. Nellie's all I'll ever look for.

JILL. You're very clever, but you're not fooling me, Henry. I've met your kind before, really I have.

HENRY. Where was that?

JILL. In the zoo. Caged. Just where you ought to be . . . ! I'm on to you now Henry, really I am, and you don't frighten me with your looks. You may leave here the winner today, but you won't always have it your way. You just see if you do! (*A dog barks in the distance again.*)

HENRY. You're a nasty little thing, aren't you?

JILL. Not nasty, Henry, only cleverer than you hoped I'd be . . . ! (*They hear* NELLIE *coming down the stairs.* HENRY *moves to meet her in the stairwell.*)

HENRY. Hoo . . . ! Hoo, I say! Hoo, what a lovely lady . . . ! (*He leaps about the room in his enthusiasm.* NELLIE *appears wearing a pretty summer dress.*)

NELLIE. It's your going away treat. I don't know but that it'll keep you from ever coming back . . . ! I'm not a pink monkey, Henry. Sit. And you too, Jill. I'll serve this time . . . ! (HENRY *and* JILL *sit at the table.* NELLIE *serves.*)

HENRY. (*To* JILL.) I thought you were pulling my leg when you told me she had such stuff, but she does, doesn't she?

NELLIE. Those other things are only for the work I've got to do out here.

HENRY. Well you'll never have to bother about those other things again then. Not as my wife.

JILL. Oh she's going to have it cushy from now on, is she?

HENRY. Yes she is.

JILL. What will she do though while you're hunting birds and weasels in the woods? She can't lie in a hammock and watch the clouds all day. Nellie isn't built that way.

HENRY. I won't be hunting all the day, Jill.

JILL. Well that's a surprise. Did you hear that, Nellie? What will you do? Hm?

HENRY. I might take a job, so we can build up for later years.

JILL. Ohh, what kind of a job? What do you think you're fitted for? All you've ever done is hunt and loaf.

NELLIE. Jill.

JILL. And killed a few Bulgars. There's no claim to immortality in any of that . . . ! I'm glad to see you can still smile about yourself, Henry, that's a good sign for the Commonwealth.

NELLIE. Drink your soup, Jill. Henry'll be leaving in a little bit, and . . . Drink your soup.

JILL. What about your sailing plans, Henry? Have you arranged about that yet?

HENRY. My passage will be taken care of by the government.

JILL. What about Nellie's passage? I hope you're not going to make her ride steerage, like an immigrant.

HENRY. Nellie'll ride anyway she wants to.

JILL. Well that'll be nice. Do you have the money to cover any way she might want to go?

NELLIE. Jill—

JILL. Well does he? I mean how much do you know about what Henry can afford and what he can't?

HENRY. Shut up now, Jill.

JILL. I've got a right to speak about what's happening between you two.

HENRY. You've got no right, not anymore.

JILL. Nellie and I lived together and dreamed together for years. You can't throw that out like a bag of garbage.

NELLIE. Stop it, Jill!

HENRY. That's right, stop it Jill!

NELLIE. And you too, Henry! You're leaving soon. You're leaving me, and you're leaving this place. But it was Jill first got you on here, don't forget that. I wouldn't have had you stay if it had been left to me. She's the one pleaded for you, so you owe her common

courtesy if nothing else! And you still owe me respect,
Jill. I'm not stuck on a rope you can pull in whenever
you want to, and I'm not too dumb to speak my own
mind! I've said I'll marry Henry, so there's no need for
picking at one another now, nor picking over me. I'm
not a prize pig to be badgered about . . . ! Now let's have
our food down, and I'll walk you to the gate, Henry,
and wave you on your way, and hear from you again
when you're ready to come back for me.

HENRY. I've had as much food as I need. Walk out
with me now, Nellie. I have some things to say to you.

JILL. Let her finish her supper.

HENRY. Walk out with me now, Nellie. Please . . . !
(NELLIE *stands up to go. She gets a shawl from the wall
peg.*) Jill, for whatever pestiness I've caused you, I
apologize. I've appreciated your cooking, and whatever
other trouble you've been to for me, and I only hope I
can make it all up to you one day. I mean that. (*He gets
the kerosene lamp.*)

JILL. Nellie, put your boots on.

HENRY. We'll only be a minute, Jill. The wind won't
hurt her feet. (*He holds the door open.* NELLIE *steps
out, and he follows.* JILL *stays seated at the table. Lights
down in the house. Lights up in the woodshed.*)

HENRY. (*OFF.*) I don't know for sure which day
they'll give me to get back, but I'll write as soon as I've
found it out . . . Nellie, whatever Jill's going through
now she'd have to go through sometime, remember that.
If she squirms or begins to cry it'll only be to relieve her
feelings . . . (*He and* NELLIE *enter the shed.*) . . . so you
just let her do it will you, and don't fuss? You've got a
wide heart, I know you have, and there's room for all
sorts in there, but you reserve the center space for me,
do you hear? Because you're all I'll be thinking
about . . . ! And Nellie, if you'd like to stay on here for

our beginning I won't fret. I know what Jill means to you, and if you're going to be that torn up about leaving her, why then we won't do it, not untill she's accustomed to the idea. We've got woods enough here, and land enough here to make what we want of it. So if that's what you'd really like, why then you fix it while I'm gone, I won't mind. Just so we're together. (*Several dogs suddenly bark sharply in the distance, and several more join in.*) Sounds like that fox may have had a family . . . ! Come in now, Nellie. I'm going to catch you a parting present before I leave!

NELLIE. Henry—

HENRY. I've got my senses up, Nellie. I'm going to have you another fur in a flash, take my word! (*He dashes out with the lamp.*)

NELLIE. I don't want another fur—

HENRY. (*OFF.*) Come on now, before they lose the track . . . !

NELLIE. (*OFF.*) (*Following him.*) Henry, no!

HENRY. (*OFF.*) Come on, I said . . . ! (*Lights down in the shed. Lights up in the house as they enter.* HENRY *crosses straight to the kitchen for the rifle, then remembers he left it near the front door.*) You stuff your dinner in, and I'll be back before you finish.

JILL. Where are you off to?

HENRY. Your woods still need clearing, Jill. I'm going to bring you in another beastie before I go. Give us one for luck, Nellie. (*He leans in for a kiss and takes it himself, then rushes off.*) Get ready for the blast . . . !

NELLIE. What will you do when I've gone?

JILL. Die.

NELLIE. Oh Jill . . . ! I've been thinking. Suppose I didn't go to Canada? Suppose I got Henry to stay on here instead? What would you say to that?

JILL. I'd say no. Never.

NELLIE. I know you don't like him, Jill, but that way at least . . .

JILL. Nellie, no. I couldn't live in the same house with him, you know I couldn't!

NELLIE. You just said you couldn't live alone.

JILL. I can't, but I won't take him with you either. That's just what he wants. That's just what he's been after.

NELLIE. No it isn't. It's what I want.

JILL. It's what he's made you want! He's too bossy, Nellie. He's too greedy!

NELLIE. Greedy for what?

JILL. For everthing!

NELLIE. He'll have everything. I'll be here with him, and . . .

JILL. You'll be here and I'll be here and he'll be here, and as soon as he has you married, he'll start ordering the two of us about like a pair of laborers, and that'll kill me just as sure as your leaving!

NELLIE. Why should he start ordering us about like . . .

JILL. Because that's the way he is! Because he's a spoiled brat of a thing looking to prove he's a man, and he'll step on anyone and anything to make his case! You know that's the way he is, and you know you don't trust him either!

NELLIE. That isn't true.

JILL. Then why are you afraid to go with him?

NELLIE. I'm not afraid, I'm trying not to hurt you . . . !

JILL. Nellie, why are you doing this thing? You know you don't love him, that's not what it is. What hold has he got on you that keeps you from making sense about yourself? If he's an animal, you aren't, are you?

Whatever can you feel about that boy? What power is it that keeps you so tied to him?

NELLIE. I feel safe with him.

JILL. Safe?

NELLIE. Yes.

JILL. He'll eat you alive, and spew up your bones when he's done! Listen to me, Nellie, please. He doesn't care about you, he only wants you!

NELLIE. And I want him.

JILL. For what? To keep you guarded in a cave? What will you do with him? And what will he do with you? He told me once he thought you were a big dark bird. Well he's wanted to bring you down, that's all. You said that once yourself! Listen to me, Nellie, listen! Once he has you he'll begin despising you, and then he'll ignore you, and then finally he'll leave you to go hunting somewhere else! He's a fox, that's just what he is, but is a beast what you want to marry? Is it . . . ? Oh Nellie, how much do you really care about him? And about me, and about the farm, and about yourself, Nellie, about yourself? You mustn't do this thing, you'll destroy yourself! (*Sound of dogs barking again, nearby this time.*) They do sound as if they're on to something big again, don't they? Maybe a she fox. We'll still have to stand guard then won't we? And worry about our hens, and about our livelihood? But you won't dream about another fox. He's dead. Another fox won't laugh at you, believe me it won't. If it does we'll stand guard together 'till we smash in its brain! (*Sound of a shot outside.* NELLIE *is frozen for a moment.*) Nellie, you won't be safe with him. You'll be petrified . . . Call it off. Call it off before it's too late . . . ! (*The door opens and* HENRY *enters.*)

HENRY. I missed her. Blasted beast. She took off before I could sight her again! (*He stands the rifle up behind the front door.*) I missed your present, Nellie. I'll get it on my trip back. Are you ready to walk me out?

NELLIE. Henry. I have something to say to you.

HENRY. Say it.

NELLIE. Jill and I know each other, and we've made a life here together. And even if it can't last forever, it is a life while it does last. On what grounds can I marry you . . . you're an absolute stranger to me. So I'm asking you to call it off. Before either of us makes a fool of ourselves. And that's it.

HENRY. Is it?

NELLIE. I'm sorry, but yes it is.

HENRY. Was it the shooting changed your mind?

NELLIE. No.

HENRY. Was it anything I said?

NELLIE. No.

HENRY. What was it then?

NELLIE. I just suddenly came to my senses, Henry, and now I'm trying to keep us from making a terrible mistake with one another.

HENRY. You just came to your senses, did you?

NELLIE. Yes.

HENRY. How did that happen?

NELLIE. I don't know.

HENRY. Yes you do.

NELLIE. No I don't, Henry. Honestly.

HENRY. I'll tell you then. It was Jill, wasn't it? She found something to say to you about me, didn't she?

JILL. Nothing that wasn't plain to see.

HENRY. And if it was so plain why didn't you see it alone, Nellie? I'll tell you that, too. Because you wanted me. You wanted me, and you needed me, and you wanted me to want you!

JILL. That isn't true!

HENRY. Don't yap about what you don't know, Jill.

JILL. I know.

HENRY. Shut your mouth now!

NELLIE. Don't yell, Henry.

HENRY. She's the one tried to make sense for you, isn't she? Without her you'd have taken me for what I am!

JILL. What are you?

HENRY. I'm a man, Jill, with a man's mind and a man's appetites!

JILL. You're a snake, Henry, with poison in your teeth and destruction in your eyes!

NELLIE. Henry! I apologize for whatever fuss I've caused you . . .

HENRY. Nellie if you listen to her you're lost!

NELLIE. . . . but if I didn't tell you the truth now we'd both be feeling very silly soon enough . . . ! Your leave is almost up. The train'll be waiting. (*She crosses to the door and holds it open for him.*)

JILL. Bye-bye, Henry. (HENRY *suddenly laughs.*)

HENRY. Well it's been a jolly week here, hasn't it? Nothing lost, nothing gained. I had a bed, and I had five days in the country. No one's out and no one's hurt. Don't fret yourself, Nellie, I'll ease my mind. Too much living too soon for a soldier boy just home from the wars! I'll get my bag and be gone in a flash . . . ! (*He crosses for his bag, under the stairwell, then stops by the open door.*) I wish you'd let me take you out that last time I asked though, Nellie. One of you is going to need what I can teach . . . (*He drops his pack and hat, then reaches behind the door for the rifle. He points it at* JILL.) Have you ever handled a gun at all, Jill?

JILL. (*Backing away.*) Yes I have. Why?

HENRY. (*He lowers the gun, but moves in her direction.*) Have you ever been able to bring anything down with it?

JILL. A squirrel once, and then . . .

HENRY. A lying-down squirrel I'll bet.

JILL. He was on the move.

HENRY. But he'd just gotten up from a nap hadn't he? How many shots did you need to get him dead?

NELLIE. You'll miss your train, Henry. (*He suddenly swings the gun round at* NELLIE *and she backs up a little.*)

HENRY. This is a big point, Nellie. There's a world of difference between looking down a sight to kill, and just hoping to catch what you're after.(*He points it again at* JILL *without even looking at her.*) I don't think Jill knows that. That's what I've got to get across. (*Then again he lowers the barrel.*) When you hold a gun, Jill, you've got all the power on this earth at your fingertips, but when you aim you've got to aim with your will, or it's no use. That's what I was telling you once, Nellie, remember? (*He points the gun at* NELLIE *for a moment, then drops it back down.*) Look now, let me see what I can find to show you . . . (*He looks around the room, seemingly about to aim at some object or other.*)

JILL. Henry, don't point that thing in here!

HENRY. My hand is off the trigger, Jill, wait now . . . ! (*He slowly pivots past* JILL, *off toward the kitchen, then suddenly swings and points the gun at* NELLIE.) See, I've found Nellie!

JILL. Henry, stop it!

HENRY. (*He quickly swings the rifle at* JILL, *then back to* NELLIE.) Don't move, Jill! (*He stands holding the rifle at* NELLIE *and begins a quick series of stalking movements as he speaks.*) Now suppose Nellie was a rabbit, or a big bird, and suppose I was to begin thinking about smashing her down with a bullet. Now if Nellie was that bird, and she was alive instead of standing frozen, she'd feel my mind beginning to fasten on hers, and before it got too big a hold, she'd start to run. And when she did that, that'd be the time to catch her. Right then. Hoo! (*He quickly brings his hand to cock the gun and puts his finger on the trigger.*)

JILL. Henry! (*He snaps the gun round at* JILL.)

HENRY. Hoo!

NELLIE. Henry!

HENRY. (*Swiveling back at* NELLIE.) Hoo!

JILL. (*Screaming, with a sudden move toward him.*) Henry!

HENRY. Hoo! (*In one quick move* HENRY *swings the muzzle at her and fires.* JILL *spins back with a cry then topples to the floor. She shudders once and then lies still.*)

HENRY. It was an accident, Nellie. She caught me all wound up . . . I'm afraid she's done, poor thing. It was an accident, Nellie, I swear to you. But you'll be better off without her anyway, take my word. She was too thin, too frightened. (NELLIE *drops to the floor. Her knees buckled, she gasps for air.*) I'll have to stay here now, Nellie, to keep you warm and quiet. Would you like me to do that . . . ? (HENRY *places the rifle behind the door again and moves in close to her.*) Lean your head here, Nellie. You're all in a state. (*He gathers her comfortingly against his body.*) If I'm to be your husband then you've got to listen to me, Nellie. You've got to listen to me, and you've got to tell me what you're thinking, otherwise there can never be anything real between us. You will marry me though, won't you? Won't you? (NELLIE *suddenly begins to cry.*) That's right, you let it out. I know what Jill meant to you. That's a good girl . . . ! We will live here, Nellie, and I'll show you what a farm can really be like. We'll have stock and we'll have crops, and we'll stick out so big that all the rest of the farmers'll have to sit up and take notice . . . ! All the shopkeepers'll have to sit up and take notice . . . ! We'll keep the woods free though, for evenings. Just you and me. With the stars swirling whitely above . . . ! That's enough now, Nellie. Stand up and walk me out, I've got to catch my train . . . Stand up, Nellie . . . Stand up! (*He waits and she rises. He picks up his pack and hat. He smiles at her.*) You wait for me, I'll be back . . . ! (*He leaves,* NELLIE *stands in the doorway looking about the room, and THE LIGHTS FADE.*)

THE CURTAIN FALLS

FURNITURE AND SET DRESSING
(from stage right to left)

FIRE BUCKET WITH TONGS

FIREPLACE SET (Broom, Poker & Stand)

TWO WOODEN ARMCHAIRS with flowered seat and back pads

TWO CANDLESTICKS on mantel, with CANDLE SNUFFER and TWO HOT PADS, on upstage end, and HAND PAINTED COOKIE JAR in center.

STRAW BROOM leaning against upstage end of mantel.

BOOKSHELVES with many books, and several HAND PAINTED BRIC-A-BRAC.

MARBLE-TOPPED SIDEBOARD with drawers, and cabinets down below.

PORCELAIN BOWL, hand painted, and MATCHES WITH STRIKER on sideboard.

CHILD'S SAMPLER, framed, hung over the sideboard (optional)

SMALL WORKTABLE and STRAIGHT BACKED WOODEN CHAIR. On table are a PAINT BOX, PAINTS, BRUSH, MIXING PALETTE, and a half-decorated PORCELAIN VASE. There is also a RAG in the paint box for emergency clean-up.

NELLIE'S COAT, SCARF AND GLOVES are hung on the stage left peg.

BLANKET CHEST, inside of which is a SEWING BASKET, and a partly finished EMBROIDERY PIECE.

TWO CUT LOGS on the floor of the woodshed.

LARGE TREE STUMP in center of the shed with a LONG LOG ready for cutting.

SAW hung on the wall of the shed.

SMALL SHELF

SKINNING KNIFE lodged in the wall.

COSTUME LIST

JILL:
Act I, Scene i:
   Brown wool skirt, white ruffled blouse with cameo
      at neck
   Heavy cotton stockings
   Brown lace-up shoes
   Tan wool shawl
      Scene ii:
   Change to heavier grey shawl
Act II:
   Optional change to brown blouse (with cameo)
Act III, Scene i:
   Grey wool skirt with long grey matching jacket
   Ivory Ascot blouse (with cameo)
   Grey full-brim hat with flowers
   Grey and scarlet crocheted scarf
      Scene ii:
   Optional change to black blouse with the grey skirt

HENRY:
   World War I Canadian Infantry uniform — tan wool
   Jodpurs, shirt and jacket
   Leg wrappings with work boots (brown)
   Soldier's pack
   Hat

NELLIE:
Act I & Act II:
   Wool tweed man's knickers with suspenders

Man's 1900 pale green undershirt
Sweater
Argyle wool socks
Brown work boots
Man's wool hunting jacket and scarf
Work gloves
Act III, scene ii:
Pale pink summer dress with pink ribbon sash
White stockings (with seams) and white pumps
Cameo necklace on chain

THE FOX PROPERTY PLOT

Act I, Scene i:
  Offstage R. in kitchen:
    Hot plate
    Pot for poaching eggs and heating soup
    Auto harp (or psaltrey) (Jill)
    Lit oil lamp (Nellie)
    Double barrelled shotgun loaded with ¼ charge
      blanks (Nellie)
    Silver or pewter serving tray (Nellie)
    Jam jar and jam (Nellie)
    Three handpainted tea cups & saucers (Nellie)
    Sugar bowl (Nellie)
    Tea pot (Nellie)
  Offstage, up center:
    Two pillows (Jill)
Act I, Scene ii:
  Offstage, up center:
    Lit oil lamp (Jill)
  Offstage, front entrance:
    Shot gun (Henry)
    Two pheasants (Henry)
    Four hard-boiled eggs (Henry)
  Offstage, kitchen:
    Drop leaf table (Jill)
    Two rush seated chairs (Jill)
    Iron pan with "Hot" coals (Nellie)
    Tray with bread, margerine & jam (Jill)
    Two porcelain plates (Jill)
    Three sets of silverware wrapped in napkins (Jill)
    Four poached eggs on plate with server (Jill)
Act II, Scene i:
  Onstage, on drop leaf table, center stage:
    Tablecloth

Three tea cups & saucers
Three spoons and napkins
on sideboard:
  lit oil lamp
on mantel:
  Two lit candles
Offstage, kitchen:
  Serving tray (Jill)
  Shotgun (Henry)
Act II, Scene ii:
  Offstage, front entrance:
    Shot gun and stuffed fox (Henry)
  Offstage, kitchen:
    Iron on copper pot with handle for heating water
Act III, Scene i:
  Onstage in woodshed:
    Fox skin spread out on wall downstage left
  Onstage on sideboard:
    Unlit oil lamp
  Offstage, front entrance:
    Four parcels tied with string (Jill & Nellie)
    Shotgun (Henry)
  Offstage kitchen:
    Lamp oil in copper pitcher on small plate (Jill)
    Piece of bread (Nellie)
Act III, Scene ii:
  Onstage, on sideboard:
    Lit oil lamp
  Offstage, front entrance:
    Two logs (Henry)
  Offstage, kitchen:
    Bread and margerine (Jill)
    Three copper or pewter soup bowls, napkins and
      spoon on serving tray (Jill)
    Tureen with soup and ladle (Jill)

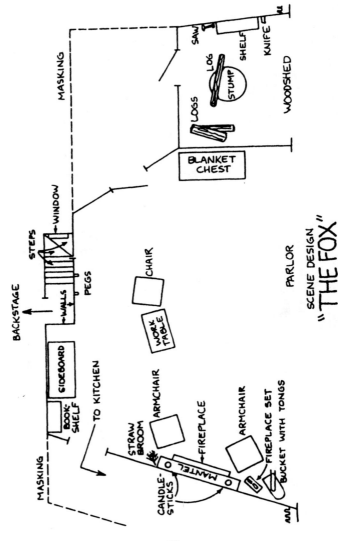

SCENE DESIGN
"THE FOX"

82

OTHER TITLES AVAILABLE FROM SAMUEL FRENCH

JACK GOES BOATING
Bob Glaudini

Full Length / Comedy / 2m, 2f / Interior
Four flawed but likeable lower-middle-class New Yorkers interact in a touching and warmhearted play about learning how to stay afloat in the deep water of day-to-day living. Laced with cooking classes, swimming lessons and a smorgasbord of illegal drugs, *Jack Goes Boating* is a story of date panic, marital meltdown, betrayal, and the prevailing grace of the human spirit.

"An immensely likable play [that] exudes a wry compassion."
- *The New York Times*

"Endearing romantic comedy about a married couple and the social-misfit friends they fix up. Witty and knowing and all heart."
- *Variety*

"Glides effortlessly from the shallow end of the emotional pool to the deep end."
- *Theatremania.com*